LAKESHORE ELEMENTARY SCHOOL

Z0102488

SO-BYB-481

Evan in the middle

This Book
Is A Gift
From...
Charlie Hyvarinen
August 28, 2010
2017-2018

Evan in the Middle

By Kelli Hicks

Illustrated by Nina de Polonia

Rourke
Educational Media
rourkeeducationalmedia.com

© 2016 Rourke Educational Media

All rights reserved. No part of this book may be reproduced or utilized in any form or by any means, electronic or mechanical including photocopying, recording, or by any information storage and retrieval system without permission in writing from the publisher.

www.rourkeeducationalmedia.com

Edited by: Keli Sipperley
Cover and Interior layout by: Renee Brady
Cover and Interior Illustrations by: Nina de Polonia

Library of Congress PCN Data

Evan in the Middle / Kelli Hicks
(Rourke's Beginning Chapter Books)
ISBN (hard cover)(alk. paper) 978-1-63430-373-6
ISBN (soft cover) 978-1-63430-473-3
ISBN (e-Book) 978-1-63430-569-3
Library of Congress Control Number: 2015933730

Dear Parents and Teachers:

Realistic fiction is ideal for readers transitioning from picture books to chapter books. In Rourke's Beginning Chapter Books, young readers will meet characters that are just like them. They will be drawn in by the familiar settings of school and home and the familiar themes of sports, friendship, feelings, and family. Young readers will relate to the characters as they experience the ups and downs of growing up. At this level, making connections with characters is key to developing reading comprehension.

Rourke's Beginning Chapter Books offer simple narratives organized into short chapters with some illustrations to support transitional readers. The short, simple sentences help readers build the needed stamina to conquer longer chapter books.

Whether young readers are reading the books independently or you are reading with them, engaging with them after they have read the book is still important. We've included several activities at the end of each book to make this both fun and educational.

By exposing young readers to beginning chapter books, you are setting them up to succeed in reading!

Enjoy,
Rourke Educational Media

Table of Contents

1
The Yard

Looking into the yard, you might think a school let the students out for recess. Kids of all sizes and ages played in the grass. Soccer balls, a baseball bat, a few orange cones were scattered everywhere.

But it wasn't the school yard. It was the Reed's backyard and all the kids playing there were siblings. Two tall blonde boys threw a football back and forth to each other. One of the boys, Jack, caught the ball, hugged it close to his stomach, and started to run. He pretended to break a tackle to the left and spun around to avoid a tackle to the right.

"You can't catch me," Jack shouted. He ducked low. He jumped high. He kept zigging and zagging, trying to make it into the end zone.

"You are so going down!" Trey reached out to grab at Jack, determined to keep him from scoring. "I have you now!"

Jack dragged Trey across the yard, his brother's toes digging into the dirt along the way. He stumbled into the end zone and dropped Trey with a THUD! The boys wrestled a bit, rolled around in the grass fighting over the ball, then got up and started all over again.

A huge tree with wide branches and thousands of soft, green leaves stood in the middle of the yard. Attached to that tree was a thin, flat piece of board. A thick rope, like the kind a pirate uses to hold the anchor on a ship, threaded through a hole in the board. The board and rope made a perfect swing. "Higher, higher," Samantha yelled. "Kick, kick, kick!" She pumped her legs forward and back, picking up speed with each motion. Her strawberry-blond pigtails swung back and forth. Samantha loved to swing and worked her legs to go up, up, up, laughing and smiling the whole time.

In the back of the yard, two small kids sat in a big pile of sand. Liam used a little green bucket to scoop up as much sand as he could. "Scoop it up, pat it down," he sang, nodding his head up and down.

He patted the top of the bucket and tried to push the sand down so he could pack the bucket until it couldn't hold anymore. "Scoop it up, pat it down," he repeated. Then, he turned the bucket upside down and dumped the sand into a pile. Sometimes, it stayed packed together in the shape of the bucket. Sometimes, the pile smushed back into a lump. Whichever way it landed, Liam yelled a loud and deep "ARRRGGG, take that!" He'd swing the bucket back behind his head, and knock the pile over. He threw his head back and laughed a loud, pirate kind of laugh, then went back to work refilling the bucket.

TJ, the baby of the group, used the flat part of his hands to smack at the sand. Each time his hand hit, he would grunt a loud "UGH!" or a "HIYA!" And, every now and again, TJ would scoop up a handful of the soft, grainy sand and pour it into his mouth.

"That's disgusting!" Liam said.

2

Evan in the Middle

Evan was the redhead in the middle of this family. *I want to play football, too,* he thought. He always tried to play with his big brothers, but his hands didn't seem quite big enough to catch the ball. It usually just slipped between his fingers. And every time he tried to grab one of the big boys, his arms swooped and swung and missed.

"You can't catch me," Jack would taunt. It always made Evan so mad!

He pushed Samantha on the swing for a little while, and watched his younger brothers.

"Push me higher, Evan," Samantha shouted.

"I'm going to push you so high, you can touch the clouds," Evan said. Samantha laughed and laughed. Evan shook his head.

Evan used to like building sandcastles, but he didn't really like the sand in his shoes and getting so dirty anymore. It

wasn't much fun to take the time to build a fantastic castle out of sand just to knock it over a few minutes later. It seemed like a lot of work for nothing. He didn't want to eat it anymore, either. So, Evan stood in the yard, too small to play with the big kids and too big to play with the little kids. Evan really just wanted to be big, but no matter how hard he tried, he was still just Evan in the middle.

3

Garbage Duty

The Reed family had a chart with chores on it. In a big family, all the kids had to help out. The big boys had the best jobs. Jack was in charge of taking out the trash. He would grab a garbage bag at the top and swing it over his shoulder.

"HO, HO, HO," Jack would shout. "Who wants garbage for Christmas?" He looked like Santa carrying his sack of toys as he marched down to the curb to leave the trash for the garbage pickup.

Trey was strong too, but he wasn't allowed to help with the trash anymore. The last time it was his turn, he was on his way out with the bag when he was distracted by some siren noises coming from his room. He found his video game loaded and ready to play, so he set the bag down and picked up the controller instead.

"What's that smell?" His family took turns asking for the next few days. When they figured out the trash was still in Trey's room a week later, they decided to give him other jobs instead.

Evan also tried to take the trash out once. "I can do it, Mom," he said. He struggled to carry the bag. He hadn't realized how heavy it was. He decided to drag it to the curb. The bag ripped and the trash ended up all over the driveway.

4

Crash Course

Since Trey and Evan weren't allowed to help with the trash anymore, Trey's job was to take the clean dishes out of the dishwasher and put them away in the cabinets. Evan wanted to give it a try. "I can do it," Evan insisted.

"Whatever," Trey said, then handed Evan a plate and walked out of the kitchen. Evan climbed up on one of the lower cabinet doors. Then he slipped. He watched helplessly, in what seemed like slow motion, as the plate turned over and over until it hit the floor with a CRASH! and broke into a thousand pieces.

Evan sighed. He cleaned up the mess. No more dishes for him.

He tried to help the younger kids put the plastic bowls away in the bottom cabinet. They just took them out again and played with them on the floor. *I want to put them away and have them stay put away*, he thought.

Evan wanted to be special. He wanted to have an important job all his own. Instead, he felt like just plain Evan in the middle. He thought if he were a little bigger and a little stronger that he wouldn't be stuck in the middle anymore.

Later that night, Evan put on his favorite blue-and-green-striped pajamas and looked up in the sky. He saw the first star of the night twinkling high in the air and made a wish. "Beautiful star, if it isn't too much trouble, could you please

make me big? I really want to be special."
He thanked the star, kissed his family
goodnight, and drifted off to sleep.

5

Big Shoes to Fill

Saturday was family day for the Reeds. The family planned to cheer on the big boys as they played in their football game, then take the little kids to run around at the park.

Evan crossed his arms and took a deep breath. "This isn't fair! What a boring day this is going to be," he said to no one in particular. Watching football when he wanted to be playing was so boring. He tried on the shoulder pads before, but they fell right down over his body. The helmet kept slipping down over his face and he couldn't see.

Evan sat on the steps trying not to be sad. He looked at the big pile of everyone's shoes waiting to be worn outside. He spied his brother Jack's cowboy boots.

Jack wore those boots everywhere. They seemed magical to Evan. They were a chocolatey-brown color with bright yellow stitching. The stitching looked like wishing stars and the boots made a clip-clop sound when Jack walked. He looked and sounded like a real cowboy.

"Why are you sitting there staring at that smelly pile of shoes?" Jack asked.

Evan didn't say anything. He just watched as Jack plopped down and tugged the boots over his feet.

"Ugh, I can't get my feet in these anymore," Jack scowled. "You want them, Evan?"

Evan's eyes got big. He wanted to jump

up and down. Instead, he calmly said, "Thanks Jack, are you sure you don't need them?"

"Nah," Jack said. "Too small."

Evan picked up the boots and slid his feet inside. They were a little too big, but Evan thought they were perfect. Evan knew just wearing the boots would make

him bigger. Although to Evan they still looked brand new, the boots had lost the deep chocolate color and seemed a bit more like grayish brown. The stitching now looked more like dirty sand than bright yellow. They barely clipped anymore. They just sort of clopped. But to Evan, they were perfect. Evan thought they were the most wonderful big boy boots! He ran outside and, even though it was daytime, yelled a big, "Thank you!" to the wishing star from the night before.

Evan wore his boots everywhere. He thought they made him look bigger and they made him feel so special. First, he wore the boots to the football field.

"Evan," Dad said, "Why don't you put on some sneakers? We can run around and throw the ball."

"No, thanks," Evan said. "I'm just going

to stand here and watch. Do you think I look tall today?" Dad gave Evan a funny look, then ran off to chase after TJ who was running away from the field.

Later in the day, Evan wore the boots to the playground. Mom said, "Evan, are you sure you don't want to take off those boots and put on some sneakers so you can climb the ladder up to the top? Don't you want to go down the slide?"

Evan walked around the edge of the playground. Looking at the playground, Evan thought the kids looked so small. Tiny, in fact. In his boots, he felt like a giant. He crossed his arms and tapped his boots on the sidewalk. He imagined that he was a giant. "Fee, Fi, Fo, Fum," he said in a giant voice. He clopped his way around the park, lifting his feet high and stomping them down on the ground.

One time, he lifted his foot so high that his boot almost fell off.

He was so busy being a giant, he barely heard Mom calling to him. "Evan," Mom said, "why don't you stomp over to the car and help me get the lunches?" Evan clopped and stomped all the way to the van and his mom handed him one bag.

"It's okay, Evan, I can carry the rest." Evan's giant smile turned upside down. He felt himself shrinking. Mom turned and looked at Evan. She tilted her head to one side. "You know what," she said, "I'm not sure I can carry all of this. Do you think you could carry a few more?" Evan was a giant again. He carried all the food to the table. It did get a little heavy, but he did it all by himself.

6
Anyone Need a Lifeguard?

Once the family arrived home, the kids headed out to the backyard. Jack and Trey started a new game of dragging Trey across the yard.

"I'll get you this time," Trey yelled.

"We'll see about that," Jack replied.

"Push me to the clouds Evan," Samantha squealed. Evan pushed Samantha on the swing until she was soaring high, giggling the whole time. Evan decided to check on the little boys. Since he was big in his boots, he thought that it was the right thing to do. He wore his boots in the sandbox. He imagined

that they were at the beach. Liam and TJ were there in the sand, and he was a lifeguard. His boots made him so tall that he didn't even need to sit up in the lifeguard stand.

He stood right there on the edge, ready to leap into action to help anyone who might get buried, or choke on too much sand. Liam interrupted his thoughts.

"Evan, why are you wearing boots in the sand? Why don't you take off your boots? Then you can feel the sand squishing between your toes." Liam pushed his toes as far apart as he could then squeezed them together so the sand could get between every toe.

Evan thought about that for a minute. Then remembered he was too big for the sand and he was busy watching them play. And anyway, he was a lifeguard, after all.

7

Sharks and Boots

The next day, the family piled in the van to go to a party to celebrate their cousin's sixth birthday. When the family arrived, kids were running everywhere. There was a great deal of noise, streamers, balloons, and even more noise. Hula hoops swung around hips, bean bags flew through the air, wrapping paper littered the floor, and frosting coated the top lips of most of the kids.

One of the cousins yelled, "Hey guys, let's go swimming!"

The kids shouted, "Yes," and "Yahoo," and "Mom, can I swim?" Everybody

changed into bathing suits and left their shoes in the house.

Evan put on his favorite bathing suit with sharks all over it. Hammerheads, nurse sharks, even a great white swam around his legs. It was fishy, scary, and wonderful all at the same time. He threw a towel over his shoulder and headed out to the pool.

"Evan, why are you wearing boots and a bathing suit?" His brother Trey looked at him strangely. "Why don't you take your boots off and put on these flippers so you can swim like a fish?" Evan thought for a minute, then shook his red head and jumped into the pool with the boots on. Trey put the flippers on and jumped into the water too.

8
It's in the Bag

Evan wore his boots in the bathtub. He wore them to the soccer field. He even wore them to bed. No one thought Evan would ever take off his boots.

"I'm worried about Evan," Mom said.

"He acts so serious all the time. He doesn't seem to play anymore," Dad said.

"His feet stink!" Jack said. Mom and Dad both looked at Jack to scold him, but Jack was right. Nobody really knew what to do.

The family went to Grandma's house the next night for dinner.

"Evan, do you think you could help me

for a little bit?" Grandma asked.

"I'll help," Jack said.

"Thank you, Jack, but Evan is the big boy I need right now." Jack shrugged his shoulders and went to find Trey. Grandma put a stool in front of the counter. Together, she and Evan rolled out dough to make biscuits. She let Evan pour the flour on the counter, not minding at all

about the cloud that floated around them. She let Evan use the cutter to make little circles. It didn't matter that the shapes weren't perfect.

"Now Evan," said Grandma, "Tell me about these wonderful boots."

Evan wasn't quite sure what to say. He liked feeling big, and he really did feel special, but he hadn't played any games in more than a week. He hadn't gotten dirty in the yard, or ridden his bike. He was too busy being Evan in the boots to be Evan in the middle.

Evan hoped Grandma would understand. He told Grandma about feeling little, wanting to be big, being a giant and a lifeguard, and how the boots helped him do all those things. Grandma sat down at the kitchen table and patted the chair next to her. Evan sat and looked at his Grandma.

"Evan, you are so special. Not because of being big or small or because of your boots. It is because you are Evan, and wonderful, and being in the middle makes you that way." She hugged him close, then went back to finish up dinner.

"Oh, by the way," she said. "There is something for you in the bag by the door, if you are interested."

Evan was curious. He sat for a moment. Then he couldn't stand it anymore and ran to the bag. I wonder what it is, he thought to himself. He reached inside and felt something rubbery. He pulled the surprise up and out of the bag.

New boots! Evan could tell they were specially made for middle-size boys just like him. They were green, rubbery, and perfect for jumping in puddles. Mom and Dad, Grandma, even his aunts, uncles, and cousins held their breath and waited. Evan looked down and took a deep breath. Finally, slowly, he slid off his old boots. He pushed his feet down into the new boots. He walked around a little, tapped his toes, and gave a little jump. He thought they were just right. Evan smiled, threw open the door, and ran outside looking for puddles.

Everyone looked out the window and watched Evan enjoy his new boots. "He's a wonderful boy," Grandma said.

"He pushes me on the swing," Samantha said.

"He's going to be a great football player," Jack said.

While the family watched out the window and talked, Evan's little brother, Liam, looked around the room. He quietly walked over to Jack and Evan's old boots,

slid his feet inside, and grinned a huge, happy grin.

Reflection

My name is Evan and I am the middle child in a large family. I love my brothers and sister, but it can be hard to stand out. I didn't think being in the middle was much fun. I looked at the little kids and remembered the fun of being so small, but all I really wanted was to be big like my oldest brothers. They seemed to be so important and have the most responsibility. I finally realized I am special just because I'm me. I have time to be bigger and I am happy being just who I am, Evan in the middle!

Discussion Questions

1. How do the illustrations help tell the story?

2. How does Evan's character change in the story?

3. What is the main message in the story?

4. Why does Evan want to be big?

5. What information does the author include at the beginning of the story that helps you understand the rest of the story?

Vocabulary

Try practicing these words using a muffin tin. Write each word on a slip of paper and place in a muffin tin. Throw a small ball or bean bag into the tin. Say the name of the word where the ball lands. Tell the definition of the word and use it in a sentence.

appealing
considerate
curious
distracted
end zone
helplessly
lifeguard
unexpected

Writing Prompt

Can you remember a time when you felt like you didn't fit in? Write a short story to tell about that time. How did it feel? What did you do to overcome the problem?

Q & A with Author Kelli Hicks

Do you have siblings?
I grew up in a family that had five kids. I was the oldest daughter, second from the top. My sister Kate was like Evan in the middle. Every kid in a big family has to find what makes them special, and every kid in my family definitely has different skills and talents.

What do you want your readers to know about having siblings?
It can be really tough to have siblings, especially when you are in a big family. You have to learn how to share and compromise. Your brothers and sisters can make you crazy sometimes, but can also be your most favorite people in the world.

Do you have kids?
I have two children, but they are seven years apart, so there is not a middle child. They have very different interests and personalities. They try to ignore each other most of the time, but they definitely love and care for one another. I am sure as they get older they will appreciate each other more and more.

Connections

Do you have siblings? If you do, make a list of fun and interesting things that you want to do together. Can you make homemade ice cream? Have a bike wash in your neighborhood? Camp out in your backyard? See how many activities you can come up with and then check them off your list if you complete them. If you are an only child, make a list with a group of your best friends.

Websites to Visit

www.simplyinorder.com/uploads/100_ Things_to_Do_When_Your_Kids_ Say_Im_Bored.pdf

http://pbskids.org/games/teamwork

http://kidshealth.org/parent/positive/ family/sibling_rivalry.html

About the Author

Kelli Hicks lives in a world surrounded by noise and activity. The second oldest child in a family of five, Kelli's life is full of family gatherings, soccer tournaments,  music, and chasing one very energetic naughty dog. Being a quiet person herself, she finds peace curling up in a comfy chair with a blanket and reading. She is a teacher and writer who lives in Tampa, Florida, with her husband, two kiddos, one sweet golden retriever, and one spirited and wild Vizsla dog.

About the Illustrator

Nina de Polonia is a self-taught artist born in the Philippines in 1985. She has loved drawing ever since she could hold a pencil. She works digitally using Photoshop and her trusty Cintiq. But the magic starts with a sketch using pencil and loads of paper. She also incorporates lots of textures done in traditional media to achieve a more organic look. She loves illustrating stories and characters that are cute, playful, and quirky.